William Montgomery Clemens

A Ken of Kipling

Being a biographical sketch of Rudyard Kipling

William Montgomery Clemens

A Ken of Kipling
Being a biographical sketch of Rudyard Kipling

ISBN/EAN: 9783337011963

Printed in Europe, USA, Canada, Australia, Japan

Cover: Foto ©Raphael Reischuk / pixelio.de

More available books at **www.hansebooks.com**

A Ken of Kipling

BEING
A BIOGRAPHICAL SKETCH OF
RUDYARD KIPLING, WITH AN
APPRECIATION AND SOME
ANECDOTES .· .· .· .· .· .· .· .· .·

By

WILL M. CLEMENS

AUTHOR OF

"Theodore Roosevelt, the American," "The Life of Mark Twain," "The Depew Story Book," etc., etc.

NEW AMSTERDAM BOOK COMPANY
156 FIFTH AVENUE . . . NEW YORK
MDCCCXCIX.

To

"A Colonial Policy of Expansion," whereby
Great Britain gave to the world a
Rudyard Kipling, this little
book is solemnly
dedicated.

ILLUSTRATIONS

ILLUSTRATIONS

Photogravure Portrait of Rudyard Kipling
Frontispiece

Mr. Kipling's House at Brattleboro, Vt.

An Original Illustration by Rudyard Kipling

CONTENTS.

A KEN OF KIPLING.

I.

KIPLING THE MAN.

In Bombay—

> "Between the palms and the sea,
> Where the world-end steamers wait,"

Rudyard Kipling was born in 1865, on the thirtieth day of December. His father, John Lockwood Kipling, an English artist holding an official position in India, was a native of Burslem in Staffordshire. He was the eldest son of the Rev. Joseph Kipling. The early years of his life he spent in the Burslem potteries as a modeler and designer of terra cotta. He was a clever young man, a great reader, a true artist, though somewhat eccentric. He attended a picnic one day with the other young people of the neighborhood, at a pretty little English lake between the villages of Rudyard and Bushton, not far from Burslem. John Kipling there met a pretty English girl, Alice Macdonald, the daughter of the Rev. G. B. Macdonald, a Wesleyan minister at Endon. He fell in love with her at once. They met very often, and their engagement was soon after announced. Then John went to the art schools in Kensington, and was afterward sent out to direct the art schools of Bombay. When he went to India he took pretty Alice Macdonald along as his wife.

As professor of architecture and sculpture at the School of Art in Bombay, Mr. Kipling produced some very able students. He instructed his pupils more especially in modelling, that when the time came he might have a staff of able men to assist him in the work of making casts of the mythological sculpture of the old and celebrated rock-cut temples of the central provinces of India. This laborious and difficult task occupied Mr. Kipling and his staff for several years, and the results of their labors are now to be seen at the South Kensington and many of the other great museums throughout the world. In 1881 Mr. Kipling was appointed curator of the government museum at Lahore, and here he accomplished great results during the years that he held this honorable position. In 1891, Mr. Kipling published a volume entitled " Beast and Man in India."

Mr. Kipling's wife, the mother of Rudyard, was a woman of great beauty

11

and charm. She was one of three sisters noted for their intellect and culture, all of whom married distinguished Englishmen and artists. One became the wife of Sir Edward Poynter, who succeeded Sir John Millais as president of the Royal Academy, while the other married Sir Edmund Burne-Jones.

When Mr. Kipling and his young wife arrived in Bombay, they were assigned to their government quarters on the Maidan. These quarters were on the sites of the ancient ramparts of the citadel of Bombay, which Sir Bartle Frere had ordered removed, and the Maidan was an open park stretching between the fort and the business portion of the city.

In the course of time a son was born to the Kiplings. Their first meeting at Rudyard Lake must have been the pretty bit of sentiment of their lives, for when they named the son they took for him that of the little lake on the banks of which they first saw each other. They called the boy " Ruddie " in a familiar way, and being a first child, the parents made a great pet of him. As a lad he had unusual aptitude for learning and scorned commonplace toys, but any sort of instructive puzzle or game that required thought and intelligence appealed to him at once. Books were his great pleasure. In fact, he was quite beyond his years in intellect. He had a will of his own, as a boy, and at times asserted it in spite of the remonstrances of his parents.

Rudyard at the age of twelve accompanied his father to England, and thence to Paris, to visit the Exhibition, which was one of the chief delights of his boyhood. He enjoyed this first

glimpse of European civilization more
perhaps because of his father's compan-
ionship. They were lovers always—
this father and son—the ideal affection
being bestowed upon each other.

Mr. Kipling, since to manhood
grown, has said with modesty of his
father and mother: "All that I am, I
owe to them."

The elder Kipling, before his return
to India, placed Rudyard in the United
Service College "Westward Ho," in
the parish of Northam, North Devon,
an institution intended chiefly for the
education of sons of Anglo-Indian civil
and military officers. From his thir-
teenth year to his eighteenth, this un-
dersized, near-sighted lad was an indifferent scholar, neither a prodigy nor
a dullard. Not always at the head of
his class, nor within reach of the top
even, he succeeded, however, when he

left the college in 1882, in taking away
with him a well-earned first prize in
English literature. For two years of
his five at the college he was the editor
of the United Service College *Chronicle*,
to which he contributed many a clever
sketch or verse.

He returned to India to his father's
house at Lahore, early in 1883, and,
journalism being his bent, he became
sub-editor of the *Civil and Military
Gazette*. In Lahore, which is some two
or three days' travel from Bombay, a
large building, embowered in siris and
peepul trees, bears across its front the
legend: "The Civil and Military Gazette Press." In the office of the *Gazette*, the natives—Hindu, Mohammedan, and Sikh—labor side by side in
setting up the type and working the
machines. Eurasians and domiciled
British subjects supply the staff of

"readers," while the imported Anglo-Indians fill the editorial chairs.

In Kipling's day, the editorial staff of the *Gazette*, comprising two men, did the entire work of getting out the daily paper; and if one wants to know how Kipling worked as one of the two men who produced the *Gazette* daily, one has only to ask Mian Rukhn-ud-din, the Mohammedan foreman printer; Bahi Pertab Singh, the Sikh bookkeeper; Babu Hakim Ali, the Moslem clerk; or faithful Habibulla, the willing chaprassi, on whose head Kipling's office box came and went daily. They will tell how Kipling worked.

Briefly, the daily work of Mr. Kipling on the *Gazette* was as follows: 1. To prepare for press all the telegrams of the day; 2. To provide all the extracts and paragraphs; 3. To make headed articles out of official reports, etc.;

4. To write such editorial notes as he
might have time for; 5. To look generally after all sports, outstation, and
local intelligence; 6. To read all proofs
except the editorial matter. For a few
hundreds of rupees a month, he did the
work of at least two men.

As an outside˙ reporter he met with
many strange adventures. Probably
his most distasteful task was his mis-
sion to interview a notorious fakir,
about whom there was great religious
excitement in the Punjab, as he was
reported to have cut out his tongue in
order that it might, with the help of
the goddess Kali, grow again in six
weeks, and thus prove the verity of the
Hindu faith. Kipling never found the
fakir, but through a hot Indian day he
found himself misdirected from one
unsavory slum of Amritsar to another,
till he was sick to death of his quest.

It no doubt suited the fakir's scheme to be evasive when a sahib was looking for him, and on his return to Lahore it was a very dirty and travel-stained Kipling who tumbled into the editorial rooms of the *Gazette*.

The Duke of Connaught, then military commander of the Northwestern district of India, was occasionally a visitor to the house of the Kiplings. When he met Rudyard he became greatly interested in him, and in the course of conversation remarked: "What are you going to do, Mr. Kipling, now that you are in India again? What would you like to do?"

"I would like, sir, to live with the army for a time, and go to the frontier to write up Tommy Atkins."

The duke considered the matter, and finally gave him *carte blanche* to go to any military station in his command,

and, if he wished, go to the frontier and live with officers or men, and if at any time he required an escort he could have one; and so Rudyard was thus given opportunity to make acquaintance with Tommy Atkins. To the *Civil and Military Gazette* he contributed many of his earlier poems and stories, and the paper, having many military men as patrons, was a proper enough receptacle for his departmental ditties and earlier tales of the Indian hills. This was the beginning, but the road from journalism to literature was indeed a rugged one.

After fame had come to him, Mr. Kipling returned once on a flying visit to Lahore, and the early hours of the day of his arrival saw him, out of sheer love of the old work, sitting in the familiar office chair correcting the same old proofs on the same old yellow

paper, with Mian Rukhn-ud-din, the
Mohammedan foreman printer, flying
round the press with green turban
awry, informing all hands that "Kup-
puleen Sahib" had returned. There
also his old chief editor found him
when he came to the office.

A little volume of short sketches,
entitled "The Christmas Quartet,"
written by members of the Kipling
family, was published at Lahore in December, 1885, at the humble price of
two shillings, or one rupee eight an-
nas. There was no sale for the little
book. Mr. D. P. Masson, then the
managing proprietor of the *Civil and
Military Gazette*, of which Kipling was
sub-editor, says he could have "pa-
pered Lahore with unsold copies of the
book." The market value of the Kipling "Quartet" to-day is upward of
twelve pounds sterling.

The following year, 1886, "Departmental Ditties" appeared, the verses
having been previously published in
the *Civil and Military Gazette*. The
publication of the book was merely
local, and found few readers beyond
the British military posts in India.
The same year he published, in cheap
form for local circulation, "Plain Tales
from the Hills," "Soldiers Three,"
"The Story of the Gadsbys," and "In
Black and White."

In many ways one of the most remarkable of these early works is the
volume entitled "In Black and White,"
published by A. H. Wheeler & Co., of
Allahabad. The book is dedicated, in
a tender and reverent preface, to Mr.
Kipling's father. The elder Mr. Kipling illustrated the eight stories of
"Black and White" in a series of about
eighteen large drawings, intended for

some future *édition de luxe* of the
book. These drawings are stories in
themselves, and to one who knows the
stories lovingly beforehand, there is
a perfectly indescribable richness and
suggestiveness about the illustrations
of them. Here is the *ne plus ultra* of
the sympathetic interpretation of one
art by another. A novelist could not
cherish his own work more tenderly
than the father has cherished his son's
conceptions, and the elder Mr. Kipling
possesses technical graphic power of a
quality to which Thackeray never laid
claim. In a word, never before were
great stories so illustrated as they are
here. Only a native of India can quite
fully appreciate the drawings or the
stories, but the gems must be obvious
to any beholder.

When Mr. Kipling departed from India in 1890 for London with his collec-

tion of stories—in whose possibilities
he had himself infinite faith, although,
so his friends said, the editors of the
Indian newspapers in which he published a number of them thought but
slightingly of them and begrudged
them the space they filled—his first
idea was to publish them in America.

He went first to Hong-Kong with his
manuscripts and copies of the queer
little books he had published in Lahore
and Allahabad, and thence to San
Francisco. There he found neither
publisher nor friend, nor would the
newspapers of that city give him em-
ployment. Is it not natural then that
some years later he should write of San
Francisco as "a mad city—inhabited
for the most part by perfectly insane
people, whose women are of a remarkable beauty."

So he 'made his way to New York,

23

with a letter of introduction in his
pocket to a prominent publishing'
house. By some curious affinity in
lack of insight, this house thought no
more of the stories than did the un-
appreciative editors out in India. In
fact, they not only refused to bring out
Kipling's book, but they also, as he
thought, treated him very cavalierly
—in fact, snubbed him. Those who
know the publishers will be very slow
to believe this, as the house in question is noted for its courtesy in all its
dealings, and a highly sensitive author
is not perhaps the best judge in his
own case.

Mr. Kipling, in his disgust, made no
further attempt to dispose of his stories on this side of the Atlantic, but
sailed away for England. He tried
his luck in London with better success,
so far as finding a publisher is con-

24

cerned. His stories were brought out, but, strange as it may appear in view of their subsequent popularity, they failed. No reviewer seemed to be impressed by them—in fact, few if any reviewers paid any attention to them at all. They were piled up on the shelves of the bookseller, covered with dust, showing no prospect of resurrection. Kipling had the magnificent faith of genius in the certainty of his triumph, but every possible trial of his faith was experienced. It looked as if the triumph would be postponed until after his death, when some student of obscure literature in the latter half of the twentieth century should, by chance, light on these forgotten volumes, and wonder at the stupidity of his ancestors in leaving them to die stillborn. Kipling had friends and relatives of wealth and position in England; but he was too proud to make himself known to them in the rôle of unsuccessful author, when he had planned to visit them as a conquering hero. They knew nothing of his being in London—and, if they thought anything about him at all, supposed he was in India or wandering about in some remote corner of the world. Kipling's stock of money had given out. His lodgings and board were of the most economical. It looked as if he intended to gain his living by some less agreeable occupation than story-writing.

One evening, Edmund Yates sat down to dinner at his club, wondering what would make a good stirring article for his paper—the London *World*. He asked a friend at an adjoining table if he did not know of something that was going on. Replied the friend:

"Why on earth don't you print an interview with Rudyard Kipling?"

"Who in thunder is Rudyard Kipling?" asked Yates.

The friend, who was acquainted with India and with Kipling's career there, explained that he was a brilliant young man, who knew India as few men knew it, for he had a remarkable faculty of observation; that he had just come home, bringing with him a volume of stories which he had published; that he must have with him, also, a large stock of interesting memorabilia; that Kipling was the coming man in story-telling; that it would be greatly to the credit of Yates' paper to anticipate the public in discovering him; that he would at any rate have much to say that was fresh and interesting.

The suggestions thus made quite forcibly struck Mr. Yates, and he de-

tailed one of his reporters immediately
to interview Kipling. The reporter
had some difficulty in finding Kipling,
for his lodgings were obscure and his
disgusted publishers had not kept close
track of his address. But found he
was at last, and when found he had all
the hauteur of confident genius when
most prosperous, in being, on the
whole, rather unwilling to submit to
the advertisement of an interview.
The reporter prevailed upon him to do
the favor, and so the interview appeared, some two columns, in a much-
read paper. It created no little talk.
Among others who read it with interest
was the book reviewer of the London
Times. He remembered in an indis-
tinct way that Kipling's stories had
come to his desk, and that he had let
them lie there. He hunted them up,
and, in the light of what he now knew

28

about the man, was greatly impressed
by them. He gave them a half-column
review or more, and that with a great
many Englishmen was enough. To
find Kipling indorsed in the *Times* immediately set them to work reading
them. The stories no longer lay, dust-
covered, on the publisher's shelves.
The stock on hand was not sufficient
to meet the sudden demand, and the
young man from India was at once a
much-discussed author.

Fame came with the reappearance of
" Departmental Ditties " and " Barrack-
Room Ballads." In these virile poems,
as a reviewer said: " The seamy heroes
sang of the life they lived with all their
dramatic virtues as well as their dra- .
matic sins. The rugged strength of
the handling and the brilliance of the
color were recognized."

His acquaintance with Mr. Wolcott

Balestier, and his collaboration with
that promising young American in the
writing of "The Naulahka," brought
him to America again in 1891. The
Balestiers lived on a farm in Vermont
near Brattleboro, and Mr. Kipling, evidently taken with America and American ways, fell in love with Mr. Balestier's sister, Carolyn. They were
married in All Souls' Church, Portland
Place, London, on January 18, 1892,
returning to Brattleboro soon after.

When this "Avatar of Vishnuland,"
as some one has called him, built for
himself an American home on the
mountain slopes near Brattleboro, he
was already a known figure in the
world's literature. Making his home
first in a rented cottage near the site of
the house he built, he completed there
his "Many Inventions" and wrote some
of the poems of "The Seven Seas."

MR. KIPLING'S HOUSE AT BRATTLEBORO', VERMONT

The Kipling house, near Brattleboro, is a long, low building, with projecting roof that has just the suggestion of a thatch. A wide veranda extends along one entire end of the house. A long hall divides the house in the middle, there being eleven rooms on either side of the hall. The house looks not unlike an Indian bungalow. It is built on a hillside overlooking the Connecticut river, and the only entrance is in the rear. At every approach to the house is to be found the sign, " No trespassing on these grounds."

The death of young Balestier, whose light went out far too soon, was a personal loss to Mr. Kipling—a loss that he felt keenly for some years. There was genuine love and appreciation, as well as much of future greatness, in the touching verses written to his friend and co-worker, " Who had done his work, and held his peace, and had no fear to die."

While abroad in 1897, he visited South Africa, on pleasure bent, to see new peoples and new scenes. Upon his arrival at the Cape he was greeted with a set of verses after his own manner of making. These lines were from the pen of one of his own Mulvaneys, a private soldier of the name of Wallace. Here are three stanzas from the verses as they appeared in the Cape *Times*:

"You 'ave met us in the tropics, you 'ave met
    us in the snows;
  But mostly in the Punjab an' the 'Ills.
  You 'ave seen us in Mauritius, where the
    naughty cyclone blows,
  You 'ave met us underneath a sun that kills,
      An' we grills!
  An' I ask you, do we fill the bloomin' bills?

.   .   .   .   .

"But you're *our* particular author, you're our
  patron an' our friend,

"You're the poet of the cuss-word an' the
   swear,
You're the poet of the people, where the
   red-mapped lands extend,
You're the poet of the jungle an' the lair,
     An' compare.
To the ever-speaking voice of everywhere!
.   .   .   .   .
"There are poets what can please you with
   their primrose vi'let lays,
There are poets wot can drive a man to
   drink;
But it takes a 'pukka' poet, in a Patriotic
   Craze,
To make a chortlin' nation squirm an'
   shrink,
      Gasp an' blink:
An' 'eedless, thoughtless people stop and
   think!"

While in South Africa, Mr. Kipling
was interviewed by a journalist at
Buluwayo.

"Then you're going home to tell the
public all about us in ' Plain Tales from
the Veldt'?" asked the journalist.

"No, no; nothing of the kind," answered Mr. Kipling; "so don't you run

3   33

away with the idea! Mine is only a flying visit. I'm not up here for work, and am fairly at sea in these parts. Besides, the town will have grown out of all knowledge in another twelve months."

"So on the whole you've been favorably impressed, Mr. Kipling?"

"Impressed! I have never been so impressed with any community in the whole world."

The interviewer thus wrote of him in the Cape *Times:* "He takes his work hard. He is tremendously in earnest about it; anxious to give of his best; often dissatisfied with his best. He is quite comically dissatisfied with success; quite tragically haunted by the fear that this or that piece of work, felt intensely by himself in writing and applauded even by high and mighty critics, is in reality cheap and shoddy

34

in execution, and will be cast in damages before the higher court of prosperity."

Mr. Kipling's well-known story "007" is reminiscent of an experience of his at the Cape, where one of his pleasures was riding on engines. He got a permit to ride on the locomotives of the Cape Government railways, and made use of it.

An engineer on one of the roads reported that he was not up to schedule time because he carried "one of those literary swells," who had insisted on running the engine.

"He really does know something about it," declared one of the road superintendents. And in this knowing something about everything he writes lies his great success.

During his residence in 1898 in England, Mr. Kipling occupied a house at

35

Rottingdean, a quiet little Sussex village near the sea. It is called the Elms, from its surroundings of beautiful elm and ilex trees. In this quiet retreat he led the ideal life of the English gentleman, varying his routine of work and reading by a ride of three hours every morning in the quiet English lanes and byways, and walking four or five hours later in the day.

In February, 1899, Mr. Kipling, accompanied by his family, returned to the United States for a month's holiday. He was met in New York harbor by a most unexpected and complimentary reception. As his ship, the *Majestic*, ice-coated and laboring in the rough sea, neared the land, Mr. Kipling leaned over the starboard rail, watching intently three men in oilskins in a cockle-shell of a boat. They were the pilots coming aboard to take

the huge vessel into port. When the
little boat veered off, the men rested
on their oars. One of them looked up
and saw Kipling. Taking off his oil-
skin hat, he shouted, in a voice heard
above the tempest:

"By sport of Winter weather
   We're watty, strained and scarred,
From the kentledge on the kelson
   To the slings upon the yard,
The ocean's had her will of us
   To carry all away."

Then he added: "Hurrah for Mulvaney and the boys of Lungtungpen!"
Mr. Kipling stood for a moment mo-
tionless in astonishment. Then he
took off his cap and waved it to the pilot. He realized that even pilots have
books aboard their boats, and many
hours to while away at sea.

As the *Majestic* entered New York
bay, Mr. Kipling met his favorite enemy—the newspaper reporter. He met

a dozen of him, each clamoring for an interview. He denied them all, and said nothing save a characteristic bit, thus: "Every effort of art is an effort to be sincere. There is no surer guide, I am sure, than the determination to tell the truth that one feels."

The newspaper men left, singing softly, says the New York *Mail and Express:*

We've met with many men from over seas,
  An' some of 'em was shy an' some was not.
The Frenchman and the German and Chinese,
  But Kipling was the hardest of the lot.
Some of 'em talked in English an' the rest
  Would talk from early winter to the fall,
But the Mowgli-man we found the greatest pest.
  For the bloomin' sod 'e wouldn't talk at all.
Still, 'ere's to you, Rudyard Kipling, you es-
  cape our anger's ban,
You're a cold, concentered Briton, but a first-
  class writin' man.
Although you need to thaw a bit, to you we
  must be fair.
You are the master-writer, though you didn't
  treat us square.

'E 'asn't got no paper of his own,
  An' so with us 'e doesn't sympathize,
Yet we can certify the skill 'e's shown
  In 'andlin' literary merchandise.
If 'e'd only start 'is Fuzzy-Wuzzy gush,
  And cast loose 'is Anglo-Hindu talkin' gear,
An 'appy day with Rudyard on the rush
  Would last an 'ealthy journalist a year.

Then 'ere's to you, Rudyard Kipling, an' ye're
    welcome to the town,
You are a prince of writing-men, although you
    turn us down.
We give you your certificate an' if you want it
    signed,
We'll come an' 'ave a chin with you when you
    are more inclined.

Mr. Kipling shuns publicity and
observation. As a literary lion he
seldom ventures from his lair, and
declines always to be lionized. In England he has lived in retirement, protected himself against interruption of
labor, avoided social distractions, and
seldom is seen in London. When his
presence has been secured as a drawing
card for a luncheon or a dinner, he has

39

come late and gone early, and has seemed indifferent to the interest taken in him. Reserve and seclusiveness are his characteristic traits.

Versatility is the one marvel of the man and his work. As Shakespeare knew the science of expression and possessed a wondrous mastery over mere words, so Mr. Kipling knows men, animals, and inanimate things. Nothing seems ever to escape his far-seeing, deep-searching eyes—and even then he looks through glasses. Some writer has truly said: "He is a man who sees more with the same number of eyes, hears more with the ordinary complement of ears, than any Anglo-Saxon mortal has ever seen or heard or been able to express before."

He is the one writer of English at the present moment who satisfies quite fully the two great classes of readers

—the multitude, on the one hand, who read to be amused; and the cultured minority, who read for art's sake.

Devoted to his home life, domestic in tastes, simple in his habits, regular and systematic in his work, Mr. Kipling is a quiet, industrious, unobtrusive man, deeply in earnest. In his movements he is quick and lively, and, perhaps, somewhat nervous; and has a thoroughly southern temperament. Distrustful as he is about himself, he is without bounds in his recognition of others. Sir Edward Russell has described him as a " practical, spruce, athletic, well-groomed, little figure—making a splendid living—not an Amos or an Isaiah."

HIS WORK IN PROSE AND VERSE.

When Mr. Kipling first emerged from his native jungles and threw his new bright light on the civilization of England and America, the Puritans of literature were momentarily shocked. This young man from far away Lahore was neither Christian nor Oriental, nor again Occidental. His was not the polite literature of the drawing-room, nor the æstheticism of the studio; rather he reeked of the army canteen, he gave Letters an odor of horse and stable; there was too much of beer and too much of barracks and bar-room in his verse and in his prose.

The old bookworms, the classic college mummies, and the prim old maidens who wrote sonnets and went about the land organizing Browning clubs, declared Mr. Kipling's only aim was to write something that would "take" with the English people, and he would not last. " His characterization was never excellent, often mediocre, and sometimes abominable." " The tone " of his work "offended." It "testified to the chaos of an undisciplined soul," and thus on, to the end of the weekly reviews.

In a remarkably short while Mr. Kipling was not only universally read, but became a "fad," and the critics, alarmed unconsciously perhaps, attempted to ridicule rather than to be harsh; and I cannot refrain from repeating the plaint of the Cambridge parodist, who longed in desperation for—

"That far distant shore
   Where there stands a muzzled stripling
   Mute beside a muzzled bore,
   Where the Rudyards cease from Kipling,
   And the Haggards Ride no more."

As is usual, after ridicule came recognition, and the critics accepted him
as a man of letters, and all too reluc-
tantly bade him "sit down" and make
himself at home among them. When
they read his prose work, they were
at first bewildered; they read him
twice, and marvelled; thrice, and they
admired. When they were told how
a "tattered, rotten punkah of white-
washed calico puddles the hot air and
whines dolefully at each stroke," they
were at once choked and stifled and
were oppressed by a hundred or more
degrees of Bombay heat; or when they
read how "the last puff of the day wind
brings from the unseen villages the
scent of damp wood smoke, hot cakes,

dripping undergrowth, and rotting pine-cones," they at once sniffed the true atmosphere of the Himalaya valleys; and when "the witchery of the dawn turns the gray river-reaches to purple, gold, and opal," they felt as though "the lumbering dhoni crept across the splendors of a new heaven."

The world soon knew them, each and every one—Mulvaney and Dormer, and other privates in the ranks, Dinah Shadd, and Lieutenant Brazenose, George Porgie, Wee Willie Winkie, Bobby Wick, and the troop of Indians, Ala Yar, Jiwun Singh, Morrowbie Jukes, Imray Sahib, little Muhamid Din, and all the others.

Geographies and encyclopædias and dusty old tomes from the British Museum were sought for new notes on Simla, Lahore, Calcutta, Bombay,

Chubari, Benares, Irriwaddy, Lungtungpen, and more of them a score.

Yet even in the midst of their admiration, when they read of Gunga Din,
"the finest man I ever knew," they
were shocked once again to find him:

"Squattin' on the coals,
Givin' drink to poor damned souls."

and the British big-wigs surely must
have thrown a few fits when they read:
"'The Government should teach us to
pull the triggers with our toes,' said
Suket Singh grimly to the moon.
That was the last public observation of
Sepoy Suket Singh."

Mr. Kipling was compelled to go out
into the world and find his audience.
Once he found it, he was forced to edu-
cate his audience by brute force; and
then the literary epicures placed him,
well labelled, among the olives, and he

became "an acquired taste." To-day the supply does not equal the demand.

In the preface to "Life's Handicap," Mr. Kipling relates the advice he received from Gobind, a holy man in the Chubari: "God has made very many heads, but there is only one heart in all the world among your people or my people. They are children in the matter of tales. . . . Tell them first of those things that thou hast seen, then what thou hast heard, and, since they be children, tell them of battles and kings, horses, devils, elephants, and angels; but omit not to tell them of love and such like."

A vast deal of the material for his early work was gathered during spare hours, while he was engaged in journalism in India, and the result justifies the statement of a friend, that Kipling's memory is "so marvellous that

47

a character or a phrase or situation or idea, appealing to him, is forever after in his possession, ready on tap for literary exploitation." He says himself that his tales were collected "from all places and all sorts of people—from priests in the Chubari, from Ala Yar the carver, Jiwun Singh the carpenter, nameless men in steamers and trains round the world, women spinning outside their cottages in the twilight, officers and gentlemen now dead and buried, and a few—but these are the best —my father gave me."

There is much in method. Mr. Kipling declares, for each story he permits to reach the public eye, six other stories are thrown bravely and resolutely into his waste-basket. "It is not what you write," he says, "but when"; and he declares that "all thought is abortive speech," and that "we write in

48

letters of the alphabet, but, psychologically regarded, every printed page is a picture book; every word, concrete or abstract, is a picture. The picture itself may never come to the reader's consciousness, but deep down below in the unconscious realms the picture works and influences us."

Englished and Americanized, the barrack-room balladist and the Hindu tale spinner soon developed his dormant powers, and displayed his quick and ready handling of New York and London scenes and incidents. Chicago became as familiar to his pen as Allahabad. The Vermont horse yielded as readily to his word of command as the mowgli.

The American being of a race of a variegated and commingled ancestry, his language is therefore not a language at all—rather is what Mr. Kipling says it is, and he is quite right when he declares: "The American has no language. He is dialect, slang, provincialism, accent, and so forth."

"Mr. Kipling can now speak in many different dialects," says a captious critic; "he can imitate any one from a Hindu to a New England farmer; more than that, he can actually differentiate between the various patois of the same country. He will confront you almost simultaneously with the Kansas farmer, the Kentucky horse-dealer, the Bowery street arab, and the cottager from Vermont. There are five or six distinct voices, and you can tell at once what each is meant to represent, even though you see only Rudyard Kipling all the time."

Away up among the pine-trees of Maine, there lives a critic—even unto Maine a critic shall be given—and he speaks in no stinted words of praise when he says of Kipling's later work: "What impresses one is the wonderful prodigality of his genius, his world-wide sympathy, and his tireless imagination. To the ordinary story writer, who strikes here and there a keynote of human nature, and occasionally stumbles into a neatly turned phrase, Mr. Kipling shines as a god to a pigmy. There seems to be no end to his appreciation of the human animal, and, indeed, to his sympathy with the inanimate object, in whose depravity most of us have unflinchingly believed."

Mr. Charles Townsend Copeland, a professor at Harvard University, undertook once to wreck the Kipling idol and pulverize beneath his classical heel what the world desired most to worship. But even Mr. Copeland was just enough to say of the man he sought to

51

destroy: "Kipling can write not only
poetry, but prose in any dialect and
language, putting speech into the
mouths of horses, engines, and the animals of the jungle. Language is a
thing over which he has every control."

"Genius is rare," says a reviewer in
a public print. "Genius combined with
versatility and sympathy is more rare
still. Think for a moment of what this
man has written. Note the difference
in idea, local color, and treatment of
theme, between 'The Light that
Failed' and 'Captains Courageous.'
Is it not a wide-ranged, sweeping talent that can produce 'Barrack-Room
Ballads,' 'Soldiers Three,' and the
'Recessional'? Is it not a wonderful-
ly sympathetic touch that he puts into
his stories of child life, such as 'Wee
Willie Winkie'? Then this marvellous man turns completely round and

writes the 'Jungle Stories' and 'The Story of the Gadsbys'; and before one is done wondering if his talent has no end, he comes out with his 'Slaves of the Lamp' and 'The Day's Work.'"

A critic who carefully analyzed the stories contained in the volume "The Day's Work," comes to this conclusion: "Mr. Kipling stands so far incomparable as the master of romance; he has found for us the latest view of rail and screw, bolt and valve. He gave us escape from an atmosphere which was growing perhaps oppressively rich for the natural man; he took us out of doors, into the souse of the sea spray, within sound of the piston's tramp."

"No living writer," writes an admirer, "can equal the power Kipling possesses to present types from widely diverse but contemporaneous civilization with such striking artistic effect; his

53

perception of the real nature of each is profound and accurate. His preponderant characteristic is his incisive manner of getting at the very heart of things, and then his picturesque power of making the reader see clearly just what he himself sees. His wonderful imagination and originality is emphasized by a style that is stately and cheerful, and a precision of diction that always seems to choose the right word."

The intelligent usage of technical terms in the literary sense has become a second nature with him, and this characteristic utilization of words and phrases, popular heretofore only with the artisan and the laborer, has added a charm to his writings, which is becoming better understood by the great mass of readers. In his book, "A Fleet in Being," he confines his sketches of character to the marine and the stoker on board a man-of-war, and these pen pictures to the eyes of the landsman are delightfully refreshing. *

Mr. Kipling stands to-day the one writer of English who is proof against criticism—in the sense of the criticism doing injury to his reputation. His followers are legion, and they resent even to bitterness any attempt to belittle his creations. He has shown himself a master of verse and a master of prose. He could perhaps be a master dramatist, and the world has marvelled that he has never undertaken a play. However, Mr. Kipling is a man of sense and forethought, and it is not unlikely that he sees in playwriting the great and dangerous risk of failure. And why should he take us before the footlights? The public satisfaction would be only temporary, and soon would we be calling:

"Come you back to Mandalay,
  Where the old flotilla lay;
  Can't you 'ear their paddles chunkin' from
  Rangoon to Mandalay?
  On the road to Mandalay,
  Where the flyin' fishes play,
  An' the dawn comes up like thunder outer
  China 'crost the bay."

III.

POEMS FOR A PURPOSE.

THE awakening of the English people to the realization that Mr. Kipling
was something more than an army bal-
lad singer and a story teller was
brought about by the publication of
four poems—"The Vampire," "Our
Lady of the Snows," "The Recessional," and "The Truce of the Bear."

"The Recessional" was at once considered throughout the English-speaking world as one of the chief religious
events of the decade. It awoke an
international consciousness, and expressed the theology of the old-fash-
ioned English faith. The whole world

seemed to respond and agree with Mr. Kipling that "we are neither children nor gods, but men in a world of men." The verses made the English people realize that a religion of humanity was being preached rather than a religion of philosophy.

The Kipling poem first to attract the attention of all classes was undoubtedly "The Vampire." It was written in 1897, to accompany a picture by Philip Burne-Jones, the English artist. Picture and poem are called "The Vampire." The poem was printed in the London *Daily Mail*, in April, 1897, as follows:

THE VAMPIRE.

A fool there was and he made his prayer
    (Even as you and I!)
To a rag and a bone and a hank of hair
(We called her the woman who did not care),
But the fool he called her his lady fair
    (Even as you and I!)

58

POEMS FOR A PURPOSE.

Oh, the years we waste and the tears we waste
And the work of our head and hand
Belong to the woman who did not know
(And now we know that she never could know)
And did not understand

A fool there was and his goods he spent
      (Even as you and I!)
Honor and faith and a sure intent
(And it wasn't the least what the lady meant),
But a fool must follow his natural bent
      (Even as you and I!)

Oh, the toil we lost and the spoil we lost
      And the excellent things we planned,
Belong to the woman who didn't know why
(And now we know that she never knew why)
And did not understand.

The fool was stripped to his foolish hide
      (Even as you and I!)
Which she might have seen when she threw
    him aside—
(But it isn't on record the lady tried)
So some of him lived but the most of him died—
      (Even as you and I!)

And it isn't the shame and it isn't the blame
      That stings like a white-hot brand—
It's coming to know that she never knew why
(Seeing at last she could never know why)
    And never could understand.

His famous contribution to the poetry of the Queen's jubilee appeared in the *Times* of London originally, and has since been reprinted in every form and manner of the art typographic. However well " The Recessional " may be known, I am compelled, if only by a sense of duty, to reprint the verses here, lest we forget:

RECESSIONAL.

God of our fathers, known of all—
  Lord of our far-flung battle-line—
Beneath whose awful Hand we hold
  Dominion over palm and pine—
Lord God of Hosts, be with us yet,
Lest we forget—lest we forget!

The tumult and the shouting dies—
  The captains and the kings depart.
Still stands Thine ancient Sacrifice,
  An humble and a contrite heart.
Lord God of Hosts, be with us yet,
Lest we forget—lest we forget!

Far-called our navies melt away—
  On dune and headland sinks the fire—

Lo, all our pomp of yesterday
  Is one with Nineveh and Tyre!
Judge of the Nations, spare us yet,
Lest we forget—lest we forget!

If, drunk with sight of power, we loose
  Wild tongues that have not Thee in awe—
Such boasting as the Gentiles use
  Or lesser breeds without the Law—
Lord God of Hosts, be with us yet,
Lest we forget—lest we forget!

For heathen heart that puts her trust
  In reeking tube and iron shard—
All valiant dust that builds on dust,
  And guarding calls not Thee to guard—
For frantic boast and foolish word,
Thy Mercy on Thy People, Lord!
              AMEN.

Mr. Kipling thus describes how he
came to write "The Recessional":
"That poem gave me more trouble
than anything I ever wrote. I had
promised the *Times* a poem on the Jubilee, and when it became due I had
written nothing that had satisfied me.
The *Times* began to want that poem

badly, and sent letter after letter asking
for it.   I made many more attempts,
but no further progress.   Finally the
Times began sending telegrams.   So I
shut myself in a room with the determination to stay there until I had written a Jubilee poem.   Sitting down with
all my previous attempts before me,
I searched through those dozens of
sketches, till at last I found just one
line I liked.   That was ' Lest we forget.'
Round these words ' The Recessional '
was written."

Of the Jubilee ode, "Lest We Forget," no less a critic than Sir Edward
Russell has said: "I remember how it
seized me when it appeared; how it
startled all the world; how it was just
what was wanted — just the cogent,
lyrical, rhythmical appeal to con-
cience called for by a certain almost
debauch of national sentiment, quite

excusable, but become very flatu-
lent."

Mr. James Lane Allen asserts that
"The Recessional" is "probably Kipling's noblest and most enduring poetic
achievement," and then follows an
analysis of the poet's work: "It is virile
—nothing that he ever wrote is more
so; yet is refined—as little else that he
has ever written is. It is strong, but
it is equally delicate. It is massive as
a whole; it is in every line just as
graceful. It is large enough to compass the scope of the British empire;
it creates this immensity by the use of
a few small details. It may be instantly understood and felt by all men in
its obviousness; yet it is so rare that he
alone of all the millions of Englishmen
could even think of writing it. The
new, vast prayer of it rises from the
ancient sacrifice of a contrite heart."

63

The world saw in "The Recessional" the fearless expression of a sober, devout thought. It came as a loud voice crying from out of a multitude of voices, heard and recognized above the babble of Fleet Street, in a time of great national rejoicing among the English people.

For absolute fearlessness, vividness, and force, his next poetical production, the allegorical poem, "The Truce of the Bear," is beyond anything in our language.

The poem at once gave expression to what had haunted many minds after the appearance of the Czar's proclamation in behalf of universal disarmament. The motto is: "There is no truce with Adam-zad—the bear that walks like a man." Mr. Kipling does not hesitate to show his distrust of the motive which inspired that now

famous document, and the result is perhaps his most important achievement in
poetry. To cite from the Czar's proclamation:

"It is the supreme duty, therefore,
at the present moment, of all states to
put some limit to these increasing ar-
maments, and to find a means of avert-
ing the calamities which threaten the
whole world. Impressed by this feeling, his majesty, the emperor," etc.

Mr. Kipling tells in his own wonderful way the story of the hunter who
forbore to kill the great bear. Matun,
an old blind beggar, is in the habit of
following the "careless white men" as
they come back at night through the
Muttianee Pass from their day's shoot-
ing, showing them his horribly disfig-
ured face, and telling his story. It is
the story of a bear hunt. The bear,
Adam-zad, a prodigy of strength and

5   65

cunning, had been plundering Matun's goat-pens. Matun started out after him with an old flintlock musket, and finally overtook him — "all weary in flight." Adam-zad reared up, bear-fashion. He looked almost human. He put his paws together, as if in supplication. Matun was moved. His heart was "touched with pity for the monstrous, pleading thing." He didn't fire. Adam-zad tottered nearer and nearer. Suddenly, with one blow of his steel-shod paw, he blinded the hesitating, compassionate Matun for life. Then, grunting and chuckling, he shuffled off to his den. Matun urges the careless white men to avenge him of his enemy. He adds a counsel and a warning.

One would think, upon reading "The Truce of the Bear," that the sentiment expressed therein was but an old-time prose Kipling comment, set to the modern form of poesy. In his earlier days, in his short story of "The Man Who Was," he wrote: "Let it be distinctly understood that the Russian is a delightful person till he tucks in his shirt."

"As long ago as that," comments a writer in the New York *Post*, "he was full of the idea of the Russians coming down through the Khyber Pass, and of the 'terrible spree' there would be when the British met them. They were splendid fellows, those Russians, so long as it was only a question of fighting them like so many nomad Tartars; but when they set up for civilized Europeans, they became simply disgusting hypocrites. It is because the Czar has not only tucked in his own shirt, but asked the nations each to tuck in its own, that he loses all his charm for Mr. Kipling."

A Chicago bookish-man protested, and said it was absurd to find an allegorical meaning in "The Truce of the Bear." "Any bear hunter," wrote the Chicago philosopher, "could tell of the feeling of pity experienced when a bear about to be shot assumes that pleading attitude and expression, little less than human, by raising upon its hind legs with unlifted paws, and tottering unsteadily toward its foe."

A scholarly person of Denver thereupon took occasion to declare "that the feeling that permeates a hunter's breast when a bear rises upon its hind paws and advances toward him is not one of pity, but an irresistible desire to close the interview and hit only the high places in the landscape in retiring from the scene."

"The White Man's Burden," a still later poem for a purpose, was written

for the American, as "The Recessional" was written for the Englishman.
The title of these political verses was
undoubtedly called forth by the expansion policy of the United States, forced
upon the Government through the
somewhat unexpected results of the
Spanish-American war. Mr. Kipling's
lines:

"Your new-caught sullen peoples
Half devil and half child,"

are supposedly descriptive of the Fili-
pinos. The poet evidently seeks to re-
mind the American people of a duty
to be performed, hence admonition and
advice. He may speak as one with
authority in directing the American,
for no one in the United States knows
the character Asiatic quite so well as
Rudyard Kipling.

In a sense, Mr. Kipling in this poem
has outczared the Czar. The greatest

of the Russians advocated the disarmament of the nations as a means of pro-
moting universal peace. Mr. Kipling
believes it is the grave duty incumbent
on the white man to carry his civilization to the remote peoples and distant
regions of the earth.

The world, once civilized, would no
longer war, there being no more wild
races of men to conquer and control, no
vast areas of land to seize and hold
under an excuse of civilizing. Mr.
Kipling declares with no uncertain
voice that the "burden of the white
man" is to civilize the world, develop
its neglected resources, and build up
waste places. The white men of so
great and so advanced a nation as the
United States cannot shirk their share
of the world's burden. In truth, the
"American Recessional" is a poem
written for a purpose.

IV.

KIPLING'S RELIGION.

THE publication of "The Recessional" gave the religious element of the English-speaking people a new and clearer view of Mr. Kipling, both as a man and as a poet. When the world read his immortal lines:

> "God of our fathers, known of all—
> Lord of our far-flung battle-line—
>
> . . . . .
>
> "Lord God of Hosts, be with us yet,
> Lest we forget—lest we forget,"

the words of a prayer at once became impressed upon the mind. To Americans, the lines recalled those sacred words of Dr. S. Weir Mitchell:

71

"Almighty God, eternal source
Of every arm we dare to wield,
Be thine the thanks, as Thine the force,
On reeling deck or stricken field."

The churchman read again his
Psalms, and the words of David of old
burned upon the memory of the right-
eous:

"Oh God, thou God of my salvation . . .
Hear, O my people, and I will speak . . .
Mine enemies . . . slay them not, lest my
people forget. . . . O, Lord of Hosts, my
King and my God."

The strong, manly touch of piety
and reverence in Mr. Kipling's later
verse gives us in a way the well-
remembered devoutness of Luther
and of Milton, and at least the sincer-
ity of Wordsworth, Browning, and
Tennyson.

In his earlier work, particularly in
the "Soldiers Three," Mr. Kipling,
with the same sense of piety, wrote in
his introduction:

72

"I lift the cloth that cloaks the clay,
  And, wearied, at Thy feet I lay
  My wares ere I go forth to sell.
    The long bazar will praise—but Thou—
  Heart of my heart, have I done well?"

and three years later, in "Life's Handicap," this prayerful tone appeared:

"By my own work before the night,
  Great Overseer, I make my prayer.

  If there be good in that I wrought,
  Thy hand compelled it, Master, Thine:
  Where I have failed to meet Thy thought,
  I know, through Thee, the blame is mine."

There is more of a personal, abstract view of religion in Mr. Kipling's verse than an old, established faith, bound by ritual and tradition. Mr. Kipling's religion is the religion of to-day—the religion of Charles Dickens, of a broad and expansive humanity. "His religion," says an essayist in the *New World*, "is not only human, but almost exclusively masculine. It does not be-

long to saints, neither does it belong
to women, but to unchastened, faulty
men—to Dick Heldar, McAndrews, Sir
Anthony Gloster, and Mulvaney. Masculine they are to the core, like primitive heroes, with the wander-fever in
their blood, the venture-light in their
eyes, in their ears the roar of breakers
and of big guns, in their nostrils the
odors of the mossy Himalaya forests
and the spices of Mandalay to lure
them out from comforts and shelter.
The religion of such men is short and
swiftly told. A simple religion, as
simple as that of the primitive heroes
—of Ulysses, of Sidney, and stout Sir
Richard Grenville. Two words would
hold it all—courage and toil: courage,
the merry daring that laughs the world
to scorn; toil, the quenchless effort
to make the world obey. They who
forged this faith surely took counsel of

the world's prophets—of Joshua and St. Paul: of Joshua for the first of it, 'Be not afraid, neither be ye dismayed'; and St. Paul for the second, 'Endure hardness like a good soldier.' 'Do your work and fear nothing'—this is the gospel Mr. Kipling has ever preached, and he has preached it consistently."

His hymns are those of the bold and unlearned warrior—not the hymns of the cloistered student. In his poetic prayers to the God of All there is "no argument, no formal and ordered religion of the head, but a religion of the heart and viscera—out of the bowels of men in great conflict and great conquest, with the sweat and blood of grim primal struggle on their faces, and the words of inevitable need and dire honesty on their lips."

The same religion of humanity may

be found in Kipling's prose work, as well as in his hymns and poems. Only for the reason of the devout aspect of "The Recessional" were we reminded of his vein of religious feeling. In his "Drums of the Fore and Aft," there is much of this Christian humanity of the age in which we live, as when our author says:

"God has arranged that a clean-run youth of the British middle classes shall, in the matter of backbone, brains, and bowels, surpass all other youths."

The religion of the Kipling heroes—of his Mulvaneys, Gadsbys, and Stricklands—is that of human endeavor, of man's bravery, and man's daring. His heroes are not handicapped with long rules of prayer and repentance, of personal responsibility to God, the atonement, forgiveness of injuries, and the duty of showing mercy. They have already the teachings of the Spirit inborn, the rudiments of creed a part of their daily work and rations. "This religion," says Mr. W. B. Parker, "needs no interpretation. They who hold it are not men of speech. Words of their faith are far from their lips, as often the path of their faith is far from their feet; but at sea or ashore, they blazon the unspoken creed in unmistakable deeds. Sometimes it is in a revel of reckless adventure that makes a boy's blood tingle. Then at midnight, and naked, they swim rivers and take towns; they go into battle like devils possessed of devils; they put out in leaky hulks to 'euchre God Almighty's storm and bluff the eternal sea.' Sometimes it is in a soberer mood. Then they show their devotion to duty, as Bobby Wicks does in ' Only

77

a Subaltern,' and as Hummil does at
'The end of the passage.' Boy and
man, you will remember, both die; the
one nursing an unamiable private in a
fever-camp; the other, solitary in his
own unhealthy post, which he keeps to
save a comrade from exposure. All
this in silence, for these men are mess-
mates of toil and death. Their religion
is one of action, and yet, because they
have lived close comrades to death and
felt their own helplessness, they have
learned to believe—to believe as their
fathers did—in God and heaven and
hell."

V.

ANECDOTES OF KIPLING.

SELDOM one tells a joke on one's self; not so, however, with Mr. Kipling, who relates an amusing story at his own expense. During his stay at Wiltshire one summer, he met little Dorothy Drew, Mr. Gladstone's granddaughter, and being very fond of children, took her in the grounds and told her stories. After a time, Mrs. Drew, fearing that Mr. Kipling must be tired of the child, called her and said: "Now, Dorothy, I hope you have not been wearying Mr. Kipling." "Oh, not a bit, mother," replied the small celebrity; "but he has been wearying me."

Mr. Kipling wrote this reply to
James Whitcomb Riley, who had sent
him a copy of "Child World" :

"Your trail lies to the westward,
  Mine back to mine own place.
There is water between our lodges—
  I have not seen your face;
But I have read your verses,
  And I can guess the rest,
For in the hearts of children
  There is no east or west."

* * *

An English author visited the nur-
sery of a friend's house in Brighton, to
see the children. The sound of his
step on the stairs was hailed with a
shriek of delight, and the children
tumbled over each other in their eager-
ness to meet him. Then they stopped
short in dismay. "What's the matter?" he asked. "We fought it was
Mr. Kipling," said the youngest, with
tears in her voice. It appeared that

Mr. Kipling was in the habit of telling them stories, and they couldn't appreciate any one else's visits. Mr. Kipling is very sympathetic with childhood, and is often to be found romping with his own children.

* *
*

Miss Julia Marlowe, the actress, lived one summer a neighbor to Mr. Kipling in Vermont. At the holiday season he presented her, as a Christmas gift, one of his books, with this inscription on the fly-leaf:

"When skies are gray instead of blue,
    With clouds that come to dishearten;
When things go wrong as they sometimes do
    In life's little kindergarten.
I beg you, my child, don't weep and wail,
    And don't—don't take to tippling;
But cheer your soul with a little tale
    By Neighbor Rudyard Kipling."

* *
*

At a small party in England one evening, a young lady sang one of his

6   81

"Barrack-Room Ballads," and in the heat of her emotion she stepped away from the piano and alighted on his foot. She blushed and stammered an apology. "Oh, don't apologize," he whispered; "the corn was four toes off!"

*
*

Mr. Kipling sent Capt. Robley D. Evans, of the warship *Iowa*, a set of his works, and with them these verses:

> "Zogbaum draws with a pencil,
> And I do things with a pen,
> But you sit up in a conning-tower,
> Bossing eight hundred men.
>
> "Zogbaum takes care of his business,
> And I take care of mine,
> But you take care of ten thousand tons,
> Sky-hooting through the brine.
>
> "Zogbaum can handle his shadows,
> And I can handle my style,
> But you can handle a ten-inch gun
> To carry seven mile.

"To him that hath shall be given,
And that's why these books are sent
To the man who has lived more stories
Than Zogbaum or I could invent."

Zogbaum, I may be permitted to explain, is an artist-author, beloved by the navy.

* * *

Now must we spoil a Kipling story. The fable, ere ruin came, ran thus: Once upon a time, the father, John Lockwood Kipling, and his son, then a boy, were on a voyage, and the voyage proved too much for the father. While he was sick in his cabin, an officer appeared and cried:

"Your son, Mr. Kipling, has climbed out on the foreyard, and if he lets go he'll be drowned; we cannot save him."

"Oh, is that all?" replied Mr. Kipling, turning his back on the officer; "he won't let go."

A gentleman has been unkind enough to ask the elder Kipling whether this story was true. Mr. Kipling replied: "The only time that I made a voyage with Rudyard was when he was twelve years of age, and that only between Dover and Calais, going to the Paris Exhibition. I'm never sick at sea, and on the steamer on which we crossed I do not suppose there was a bowsprit or whatever they call it. I'm very sorry to spoil the little story, but it never happened."

.

A New York gentleman, who for a summer lived near neighbor to Mr. Kipling in Vermont, tells this story: "I was walking down the main street of Brattleboro one day, and saw Kipling coming toward me. He was dressed in a bicycle suit, and came swinging along at an easy gait. Just ahead of me there was a little Chinese laundry, and the Chinaman was standing in the doorway. When Kipling reached him, he addressed the Chinaman in Chinese and began a rattling conversation with him in that language. The Chinaman gave a gasp of surprise, but answered him, and in a few minutes Kipling had him smiling from ear to ear, and both of them were jabbering away in Chinese. I understood afterward that every time Kipling came to town, he stopped for a chat with the Chinaman. The Celestial would never tell the wondering neighbors what Kipling talked about, and when he was asked only replied: "Him welly fine man. Him welly gleat man."

.

Mr. Kipling is not ungracious. When asked by the editor of *The Can-*

85

tab, a journal published by undergraduates of Cambridge, to contribute something to its pages, he returned this genial reply:

"THE ELMS, ROTTINGDEAN, NEAR BRIGHTON,
"September 17th, 1898.
" *To the Editor of The Cantab:*
"There was once a writer who wrote:
"'Dear Sir: In reply to your note
Of yesterday's date,
I am sorry to state
It's no good at the prices you quote.'"
RUDYARD KIPLING.

Thereupon the editor consulted with his colleagues, and the result was a letter desiring to know what were Mr. Kipling's terms, and concluding thus: "So long as we have any garments left in our wardrobes and an obliging avuncular relative, we are prepared to make any sacrifices to obtain some of your spirited lines."

The author hastened to depreciate

such a sacrifice and introduced the following reply, with a humorous sketch of his unknown correspondents:

"SEPTEMBER 29th, 1898.

"DEAR SIR: Heaven forbid that the staff of *The Cantab* should go about pawning their raiment in a public-spirited attempt to secure a contribution from my pen! The fact is that I can't do things to order with any satisfaction to myself or the buyer; otherwise, would have sent you something.

"Sincerely,

"RUDYARD KIPLING."

Not yet satisfied, the young collegians begged for a photograph, and had for an answer this:

"As to photos of myself, I have not one by me at present, but when I find one I will send it; but not for publication, because my beauty is such that it fades like a flower if you expose it.

"Very sincerely,

"RUDYARD KIPLING."

Mr. Kipling tells this story of his father: "Kipling, Sr., went to pay a visit to an Indian rajah, who was about to bring home a queen. The elder Kipling had been engaged in the decorations of the palace, and its owner showed him the gifts of stuffs and perfumes he had procured for his coming spouse. The rajah also sent for his jewel caskets, and asked Mr. Kipling to assist him in selecting the gems to be included in the marriage gifts. They were of extraordinary size and value, such gems as are seldom seen except in the East, and to the artist the selection was a pleasure. Finally he lifted a wonderful diamond, one of the choicest gems in the collection, and said: 'You should send this. No woman could resist it.' The rajah looked up, caught it, and held it jealously to his breast. Then, slowly replacing it

in the casket, answered: ' Nay, such
gems be not for women.' "

.

Mr. Kipling, one night in a concert
hall, saw two young men ply two girls
with liquor until they were drunk.
They then led them, staggering, down
a dark street. " Then," he says, " I became a Prohibitionist. Better it is that
a man should go without his beer in
public places, and content himself with
swearing at the narrow-mindedness
of the majority; better it is to poison
the inside with very vile temperance
drinks, and to buy lager furtively at
back doors, than to bring temptation
to the lips of young fools such as the
four I had seen. I understand now
why the preachers rage against drink.
I have said: ' There is no harm in it,
taken moderately ' ; and yet my own
demand for beer helped directly to send

these two girls reeling down the dark street to—God alone knows what end. If liquor is worth drinking, it is worth taking a little trouble to come at—such trouble as a man will undergo to compass his own desires. It is not good that we should let it lie before the eyes of children, and I have been a fool in writing to the contrary."

* *
*

At the time he wrote "The Last Chanty" some one asked him how he pronounced it. "Well," he replied, "the really elegant and well-bred people pronounce it 'Chanty,' but those who know what they are talking about call it 'Shanty.'"

* *
*

When in New York, Mr. Kipling frequents the University Club. Being of a rather retiring sort, personally, it was a long time before he came to be well known to the majority of the club's habitués, and two of the members made his acquaintance one day in a rather odd way. The two friends went into the club restaurant, choosing a table next to one occupied by a quiet-looking man who was devouring a chop and drinking a glass of ale all by himself. One of Kipling's books had just come out, and the friends fell to discussing it with vigor. Before long they were estimating all the Kipling writings in the frankest and most ingenuous fashion. Being healthy-minded men and of good literary tastes, they both thought well of his productions on the whole, and said so plainly; yet they each had found a few flies in the amber, and they naturally talked about them. Some of the defects which they had noticed seemed to the speakers to be really serious, and one of them said

somebody ought to draw Kipling's attention to them. At just about that
time the stranger at the adjoining table
faced about, got up from his seat, and
walked over to the critics.

"I hope you'll pardon me," he said,
smiling widely upon them, "but I have
been obliged to listen to your conversation for quite a long while, and I've
become so much interested in it that
I'd like to join in. Besides, my name
happens to be Rudyard Kipling, and it
isn't fair for me to sit still and listen
without making myself known. But
possibly I'll be able to explain some
things to you, and I'm sure I shall de-
rive a good deal of benefit from your
talk."

And the three of them derived
much benefit.

* *
*

An American who was in company

NAULAKHA
BRATTLEBORO
VERMONT

And regrets that his present engagements in Vermont do not allow him to accept the very kind invitation of The Aldine Club to an Oriental Evening on the night of the 31st January.

Rudyard Kipling

Jan. 26. 1895.

AN ORIGINAL DRAWING BY RUDYARD KIPLING.

with Mr. Kipling in a ramble about London tells this story:

"One afternoon we went together to the Zoo, and, while strolling about, our ears were assailed by the most melancholy sound I have ever heard— a complaining, fretting, lamenting sound proceeding from the elephant house.

"'What's the matter in there?' asked Mr. Kipling of the keeper.

"'A sick elephant, sir; he cries all the time; we don't know what to do with him,' was the answer.

"Mr. Kipling hurried away from me in the direction of the lament, which was growing louder and more painful. I followed, and saw him go up close to the cage, where stood an elephant with sadly drooped ears and trunk. He was crying actual tears at the same time that he mourned his lot most audibly.

93

In another moment Mr. Kipling was right up at the bars, and I heard him speak to the sick beast in a language that may have been elephantese, but certainly was not English. Instantly the whining stopped, the ears were lifted, the monster turned his sleepy, little, suffering eyes upon his visitor, and put out his trunk. Mr. Kipling began to caress it, still speaking in the same soothing tone, and in words unintelligible to me at least.

"After a few minutes the beast began to answer in a much lower tone of voice, and evidently recounted his woes. Possibly elephants, when 'enjoying poor health,' like to confide their symptoms to sympathizing listeners as much as do some human invalids. Certain it was that Mr. Kipling and that elephant carried on a conversation, with the result that the ele-

phant found his spirits much cheered
and improved. The whine went out of
his voice, he forgot that he was much
to be pitied, he began to exchange ex-
periences with his friend, and he was
quite unconscious, as was Mr. Kipling,
of the amused and interested crowd col-
lecting about the cage. At last, with
a start, Mr. Kipling found himself and
his elephant the observed of all observ-
ers, and beat a hasty retreat, leaving
behind him a very different creature
from the one he had found.

"'Doesn't that beat everything you
ever saw?' ejaculated a compatriot of
mine, as the elephant trumpeted a loud
and cheerful good-by to the back of his
vanishing suitor; and I agreed with
him that it did.

"'What language were you talking
to that elephant?' I asked when I overtook my friend.

95

"' Language? What do you mean?'
he answered with a laugh.

"' Are you a Mowgli?' I persisted;
' and can you talk to all those beasts in
their own tongues?' but he only smiled
in reply."

* *
*

Mr. Dooley, the American humorist,
has this to say of Mr. Kipling: "What
I like about Kipling is that his pomes
is r-right off th' bat, like me con-versa-
tions with you, me boy. He's a min-
yitman, a r-ready pote that sleeps like
th' dhriver iv truck 9, with his poetic
pants in his boots beside his bed an'
him r-ready to jump out an' slide down
th' pole th' minyit th' alarm sounds."

* *
*

Certain persons sending out a penny
magazine called the *The School Budget*, intended for the enlightenment
of Horsmonden School in Kent, asked

Rudyard Kipling to write something for them, the rate to be paid him being 2s. per one thousand words. The editors quoted Kipling's lines:

"The song I sing for the good red gold
The same I sing for the white money;
But the best I sing for the clout o' meal
That simple people give me."

If he did not write for them at the rate of 2s. per one thousand words, the publishers said they would score him in their very next issue. Mr. Kipling evidently was alarmed, for he sent them the following:

"Easter Monday, 1898.

" *To the Editors School Budget:*

"GENTLEMEN: I am in receipt of your letter of no date, together with a copy of *The School Budget*, February 14; and you seem to be in possession of all the cheek that is in the least likely to do you any good in this world or the next. And, furthermore, you have

7   97

omitted to specify where your journal is printed and in what county of England Horsmonden is situated.

"But, on the other hand, and notwithstanding, I very much approve of your 'Hints on Schoolboy Etiquette,' and have taken the liberty of sending you a few more, as following:

"1. If you have any doubts about a quantity, cough. In three cases out of five this will save you being asked to 'say it again.'

"2. The two most useful boys in a form are (*a*) the master's favorite, pro tem. (*b*) his pet aversion. With a little judicious management (*a*) can keep him talking through the first half of the construe, and (*b*) can take up the running for the rest of the time. N. B.—A syndicate should arrange to do (*b's*) imposts in return for this service.

"3. A confirmed guesser is worth his weight in gold on a Monday morning.

"4. Never shirk a master out of

bounds. Pass him with an abstracted eye, and at the same time pull out a letter and study it earnestly. He may think it is a commission or some one else.

"5. When pursued by the native farmer always take to the nearest plow-land. Men stick in furrows that boys can run over.

"6. If it is necessary to take other people's apples, do it on a Sunday. You can then put them inside your topper, which is better than trying to button them into a tight 'Eton.'

"You will find this advice worth enormous sums of money, but I shall be obliged with a check or postal order for 6*d.* at your earliest convenience, if the contribution should be found to fill more than one page.

"Faithfully yours,

"RUDYARD KIPLING."

⁎

When Mr. Kipling was once asked where he obtained the material for his

wonderful story of the "White Seal,"
in one of the "Jungle Books," he answered: "I have seen it all with my
own eyes."

*   *
*

Everywhere he goes his friends be-
seech him to write Mulvaney tales.
Recently some one again questioned
him on the reason of Mulvaney's
silence, and he answered whimsi-
cally: "Terrance hasn't reported for
duty in months. Drunk again, I suppose."

*   *
*

In a published interview, Mr. James
Whitcomb Riley, the poet of the people, said of Kipling:

"A lot of fellows, who know of Kip-
ing's early history, think that he just
did it—that he just happened. But
that fellow was hustling around newspaper offices from the time he was thir-

teen years old. Born and brought up among a strange people, with queer customs, he was for years gathering material for his work.

"He has the greatest curiosity of any man I ever knew; everything interests him. In fact, he is a regular literary blotting-pad, soaking up everything on the face of the earth. Who before Kipling ever gave us animal talk? 'Æsop's Fables' were kindergarten talk compared with his. Think of a man only thirty-two years old who has given to the world eleven volumes of prose and verse! He has only just started.

"Another thing: read him from beginning to end, study him, become as familiar with his work as you will— every new bit from him displays some trait, some line of thought that is new. That man is great."

Mr. Kipling's phrasing is picturesque in the extreme. Meeting a friend once, after a long separation, he said: "Good heaven! How much water has flowed under the bridges since we two met!"

* *
*

In Rottingdean, England, where Mr. Kipling lives, there is a hotel, the White Horse by name, kept by an old gentleman named Welfare. Mr. Kipling frequently passed his evenings with this Welfare, and together they smoked and discussed politics. Welfare was a strong Radical, and Mr. Kipling an advanced imperialist. One can imagine, therefore, that these were spirited meetings. Finally Mr. Welfare fell ill. Mr. Kipling called just as usual, and he would sit by the bedside and talk. As before, they bolted politics and talked crosswise and flung their lances. It was the practice of the doctor to call quite late and take his patient's temperature, and he always wondered to find him, in what should have been the quietest hour of the day, heated and perturbed. This went on for several days—the doctor wondering, Mr. Kipling arguing, and Mr. Welfare igniting—until the maids let out the secret of the nightly discussion. Then the surgeon came to the writer's house.

"Mr. Kipling," said he, "you must call no more at the White Horse."

"Why not?" said Kipling.

"Because," said the doctor, "you are killing the landlord. On Monday when you had gone his temperature increased seven degrees, Tuesday it increased eight, and last night when I called it had gone up nine. At this rate you'll burn the house down."

Mr. Kipling sold a book to a London publisher at a price that netted the author one shilling a word. The publication of this fact came under the notice of a Fleet Street humorist, who, "for the fun of the thing," wrote to the author, saying that, as wisdom seems to be quoted at retail prices, he himself would like one word, for which he enclosed a shilling postal order. The reply came in due course. Mr. Kipling had kept the shilling postal order, and politely returned the one significant word "Thanks!" written on a large sheet of writing paper.

* *
*

Writing from Chicago, in his younger days, Mr. Kipling said:

"I have struck a city—a real city— and they call it Chicago. Having seen it, I urgently desire never to see it again. It is inhabited by savages."

Here is Mr. Kipling's delightful comment upon the daughters of Uncle Sam:

"Sweet and comely are the maidens of Devonshire; delicate and of gracious seeming those who live in the pleasant places of London; fascinating, for all their demureness, the damsels of France, clinging closely to their mothers, with large eyes wondering at the wicked world; excellent in her own place and to those who understand her is the Anglo-Indian 'spin' in her second season; but the girls of America are above and beyond them all. They are clever, they can talk—yea, it is said that they think. Certainly they have an appearance of so doing which is delightfully deceptive."

* * *
*

When Mrs. Kipling presented her husband with a son, the first male heir of the Kipling house, the event was considered of enough importance by the press to announce the fact by telegraph in the newspapers. The news reaching San Francisco, inspired a local poet to pen these lines:

KIPLING-ON-PARADE.

"What is the baby crying for?" said Kipling-
    on-Parade.
"Oh, walk with it, just walk with it," the
    Mamma Kipling said.
"What makes it yell so loud, so loud?" said
    Kipling-on-Parade.
"It wants to trot to Mandalay," the Mamma
    Kipling said.
   'E is walkin' with the baby, in the bedroom's
    'ollow square;
   The babe, it will not sleep at all, which
    makes the poet swear;
   'E's nothin' but 'is slippers on—'is face is
    full of care;
   An' 'e'll walk an' trot the baby until mornin'.

"Oh, what was it that once I wrote?" groaned
    Kipling-on-Parade.
"O' single men in barrack-rooms?" Then Mrs.
    Kipling said:

"'Twas 'Please to walk in front sir,' and Rud-
yard, I'm afraid
That the 'trouble' which you mentioned has
the baby's sleep delayed."
'E is walkin' with the baby, which is cryin'
more and more;
"There's worser things than marchin' from
Umballa to Cawnpore."
Now it's "special train for Atkins" as 'e
strides across the floor—
Oh, the baby'll go to sleep to-morrow
mornin'.

"It's cot is right- 'and cot to mine," said
Kipling-on-Parade.
"Oh, baby will not sleep, I know," the Mamma
Kipling said.
"I've walked this floor a thousand times," said
Kipling-on-Parade.
"Alas! that baby suffers so:" the Mamma
Kipling said.
Now, barrack days are in 'is mind, in spite
o' baby's yell;
An' though 'is " 'eels are blistered " an' they
"feels to 'urt like 'ell,"
'E "drops some tallow" in 'is socks, an' that
does "make 'em well."
An' so 'e keeps a-marchin' on 'til mornin'.

"Fix up some paregoric, dear," said Kipling-
on-Parade.

"We used it all two days ago," the Mamma
    Kipling said.
"Then peppermint or catnip tea," said Kipling-
    on-Parade.
"We're out of both—do walk some more," the
    Mamma Kipling said.
    An' now the sun is rising, for at last has
    come the day.
    An' 'ittle baby, gone to sleep, is smilin', as
    to say :
    'Oh, thank you, Mister Atkins, for this
    bloomin' night o' play,
    An' now I'm only sorry that it's mornin'.'"

VI.

KIPLING AND MARK TWAIN.

In 1890, in the month of August,
when Rudyard Kipling arrived in New
York a poor, struggling, young journalist, he secured a commission from
a metropolitan newspaper to interview
Mark Twain at his home in Elmira.
Thither Mr. Kipling journeyed, and
afterward, in the printed account of his
visit, he described the temptation
which had beset him to steal the great
humorist's corncob pipe as a relic. It
was a delicate touch of homage, coming
from the man who has done more than
any other to carry on the traditions
established by the American writer,

and in so doing in a large measure to
supersede him.

How quickly came the good fortune
of the British Indian and the misfor-
tunes of the American. The appearance of "Departmental Ditties" and
"Barrack-Room Ballads" soon marked
the beginning of a new sledge-hammer
pen in literature. British India moved
rapidly to the fore, and to-day Mr.
Rudyard Kipling is the ideal masculine writer, and his is the pipe
that is coveted by boys and elemental
men.

As a tribute to the journalistic labors
of Mr. Kipling, as a compliment to
Mark Twain, and to the credit of the
New York *Herald*, I append hereto the
story of Mr. Kipling's interview with
Mark Twain, as it originally appeared
in *The Herald* over Mr. Kipling's sig-
nature, on August 17th, 1890.

AN INTERVIEW WITH MARK TWAIN.

You are a contemptible lot out there, over yonder. Some of you are Commissioners, and some Lieutenant-Governors, and some have the V. C., and a few are privileged to walk about the Mall arm in arm with the Viceroy; but I have seen Mark Twain this golden morning, have shaken his hand, and smoked a cigar—no, two cigars—with him, and talked with him for more than two hours! Understand clearly that I do not despise you; indeed, I don't. I am only very sorry for you all, from the Viceroy downward. To soothe your envy and to prove that I still regard you as my equals, I will tell you all about it.

They said in Buffalo that he was in Hartford, Conn.; and again they said perchance he is gone upon a journey to Portland, Me.; and a big, fat drummer vowed that he knew the great man intimately, and that Mark was spending the summer in Europe—which infor-

mation so upset me that I embarked
upon the wrong train, and was incon-
tinently turned out by the conductor
three-quarters of a mile from the station, amid the wilderness of railway
tracks. Have you ever, encumbered
with great coat and valise, tried to
dodge diversely-minded locomotives
when the sun was shining in your eyes?
But I forgot that you have not seen
Mark Twain, you people of no account!

Saved from the jaws of the cow-
catcher, I wandered devious, a stranger
met.

"Elmira is the place. Elmira in the
State of New York—this State, not
two hundred miles away"; and he
added, perfectly unnecessarily, "Slide,
Kelly, slide."

I slid on the West Shore line, I slid
till midnight, and they dumped me
down at the door of a frowzy hotel in
Elmira. Yes, they knew all about
"that man Clemens," but reckoned he
was not in town; had gone East somewhere. I had better possess my soul

in patience till the morrow, and then dig up the "man Clemens'" brother-in-law, who was interested in coal.

The idea of chasing half a dozen relatives in addition to Mark Twain up and down a city of thirty thousand inhabitants kept me awake. Morning revealed Elmira, whose streets were desolated by railway tracks, and whose suburbs were given up to the manufacture of door sashes and window frames. It was surrounded by pleasant, fat, little hills, trimmed with timber and topped with cultivation. The Chemung River flowed generally up and down the town, and had just finished flooding a few of the main streets.

The hotel man and the telephone man assured me that the much-desired brother-in-law was out of town, and no one seemed to know where "the man Clemens" abode. Later on I discovered that he had not summered in that place for more than nineteen seasons, and so was comparatively a new arrival.

A friendly policeman volunteered the news that he had seen Twain or some one very like him driving a buggy on the previous day. This gave me a delightful sense of nearness to the great author. Fancy living in a town where you could see the author of "Tom Sawyer," or "some one very like him," jolting over the pavements in a buggy!

"He lives out yonder at East Hill," said the policeman; "three miles from here."

Then the chase began—in a hired hack, up an awful hill, where sunflowers blossomed by the roadside, and crops waved, and *Harper's Magazine* cows stood in eligible and commanding attitudes knee deep in clover, all ready to be transferred to photogravure. The great man must have been persecuted by outsiders aforetime, and fled up the hill for refuge.

Presently the driver stopped at a miserable, little, white wood shanty, and demanded "Mister Clemens."

"I know he's a big bug and all that,"

he explained, "but you can never tell
what sort of notions those sort of men
take it into their heads to live in, any-
ways."

There rose up a young lady who was
sketching thistle tops and golden rod,
amid a plentiful supply of both, and
set the pilgrimage on the right path.

"It's a pretty Gothic house on the
left-hand side a little way farther on."

"Gothic h——," said the driver.
"Very few of the city hacks take this
drive, specially if they knew they are
coming out here," and he glared at me
savagely.

It was a very pretty house, anything
but Gothic, clothed with ivy, standing
in a very big compound, and fronted by
a veranda full of all sorts of chairs and
hammocks for lying in all sorts of posi-
tions. The roof of the veranda was a
trellis-work of creepers, and the sun
peeped through and moved on the shining boards below.

Decidedly this remote place was an
ideal one for working in, if a man

could work among these soft airs and
the murmur of the long-eared crops
just across the stone wall.

Appeared suddenly a lady used to
dealing with rampageous outsiders.
"Mr. Clemens has just walked down-
town. He is at his brother-in-law's
house."

Then he was within shouting dis-
tance, after all, and the chase had not
been in vain. With speed I fled, and
the driver, skidding the wheel and
swearing audibly, arrived at the bottom
of that hill without accidents. It was
in the pause that followed between
ringing the brother-in-law's bell and
getting an answer that it occurred to
me for the first time Mark Twain
might possibly have other engagements than the entertainment of es-
caped lunatics from India, be they ever
so full of admiration. And in another
man's house — anyhow, what had I
come to do or say? Suppose the drawing-room should be full of people, a
levee of crowned heads; suppose a

baby were sick anywhere, how was I to explain I only wanted to shake hands with him?

Then things happened somewhat in this order. A big, darkened drawing-room; a huge chair; a man with eyes, a mane of grizzled hair, a brown moustache covering a mouth as delicate as a woman's, a strong, square hand shaking mine, and the slowest, calmest, levellest voice in all the world saying:

"Well, you think you owe me something, and you've come to tell me so. That's what I call squaring a debt handsomely."

"Piff!" from a cob pipe (I always said that a Missouri meerschaum was the best smoking in the world), and, behold! Mark Twain had curled himself up in the big armchair, and I was smoking reverently, as befits one in the presence of his superior.

The thing that struck me first was that he was an elderly man; yet, after a minute's thought, I perceived that it was otherwise, and in five minutes, the eyes looking at me, I saw that the gray hair was an accident of the most trivial kind. He was quite young. I was shaking his hand. I was smoking his cigar, and I was hearing him talk—this man I had learned to love and admire fourteen thousand miles away.

Reading his books, I had striven to get an idea of his personality, and all my preconceived notions were wrong and beneath the reality. Blessed is the man who finds no disillusion when he is brought face to face with a revered writer. That was a moment to be remembered; the land of a twelve-pound salmon was nothing to it. I had hooked Mark Twain, and he was treating me as though under certain circumstances I might be an equal.

About this time I became aware that he was discussing the copyright question. Here, so far as I remember, is what he said. Attend to the words of the oracle through this unworthy medium transmitted. You will never be able to imagine the long, slow surge of

the drawl, and the deadly gravity of
the countenance, any more than the
quaint pucker of the body, one foot
thrown over the arm of the chair, the
yellow pipe clinched in one corner of
the mouth, and the right hand casually
caressing the square chin:

"Copyright. Some men have morals, and some men have—other things.
I presume a publisher is a man. He is
not born. He is created—by circumstances. Some publishers have morals.
Mine have. They pay me for the English productions of my books. When
you hear men talking of Bret Harte's
works and other works and my books
being pirated, ask them to be sure of
their facts. I think they'll find the
books are paid for. It was ever thus.

"I remember an unprincipled and
formidable publisher. Perhaps he's
dead now. He used to take my short
stories—I can't call it steal or pirate
them. It was beyond these things altogether. He took my stories one at a
time and made a book of it. If I wrote

an essay on dentistry or theology or
any little thing of that kind—just an
essay that long (he indicated half an
inch on his finger), any sort of essay—
that publisher would amend and im-
prove my essay.

" He would get another man to write
some more to it or cut it about exactly
as his needs required.   Then he would
publish a book called ' Dentistry by
Mark Twain,' that little essay and
some other things not mine added.
Theology would make another book,
and so on.   I do not consider that fair.
It's an insult.   But he's dead now, I
think.   I didn't kill him.

" There is a great deal of nonsense
talked about international copyright.
The proper way to treat a copyright is
to make it exactly like real estate in
every way.

" It will settle itself under these con-
ditions.   If Congress were to bring in
a law that a man's life was not to extend over a hundred and sixty years,
somebody would laugh.   It wouldn't

concern anybody. The men would be out of the jurisdiction of the court. A term of years in copyright comes to exactly the same thing. No law can make a book live or cause it to die before the appointed time.

"Tottletown, Cal., was a new town, with a population of 3,000—banks, fire brigade, brick buildings, and all the modern improvements. It lived, it flourished, and it disappeared. To-day no man can put his foot on any remnant of Tottletown, Cal. It's dead. London continues to exist.

"Bill Smith, author of a book read for the next year or so, is real estate in Tottletown. William Shakespeare, whose works are extensively read, is real estate in London. Let Bill Smith, equally with Mr. Shakespeare now deceased, have as complete a control over his copyright as he would over real estate. Let him gamble it away, drink it away, or—give it to the church. Let his heirs and assigns treat it in the same manner.

" Every now and again I go up to
Washington, sitting on a board to drive
that sort of view into Congress. Congress takes its arguments against international copyright delivered ready
made, and—Congress isn't very strong.
I put the real-estate view of the case
before one of the Senators.

" He said: ' Suppose a man has written a book that will live forever?'

" I said: ' Neither you nor I will ever
live to see that man, but we'll assume
it.   What then?'

" He said: ' I want to protect the
world against that man's heirs and
assigns working under your theory.'

" I said: ' You think all the world
are as big fools as ——, that all the
world has no commercial sense.   The
book that will live forever can't be
artificially kept up at inflated prices.
There will always be very expensive
editions of it and cheap ones issuing
side by side.'

" Take the case of Sir Walter Scott's
novels," he continued, turning to me.

"When the copyright notes protected them, I bought editions as expensive as I could afford, because I liked them. At the same time the same firm were selling editions that a cat might buy. They had their real estate, and not being fools, recognized that one portion of the plot could be worked as a gold mine, another as a vegetable garden, and another as a marble quarry. Do you see?"

What I saw with the greatest clearness was Mark Twain being forced to fight for the simple proposition that a man has as much right in the work of his brains (think of the heresy of it!) as in the labor of his hands. When the old lion roars, the young whelps growl. I growled assentingly, and the talk ran on from books in general to his own in particular.

Growing bold, and feeling that I had a few hundred thousand folk at my back, I demanded whether Tom Sawyer married Judge Thatcher's daughter and whether we were ever going to hear of Tom Sawyer as a man.

"I haven't decided," quoth Mark Twain, getting up, filling his pipe, and walking up and down the room in his slippers. "I have a notion of writing the sequel to 'Tom Sawyer' in two ways. In one I would make him rise to great honor and go to Congress, and in the other I should hang him. Then the friends and enemies of the book could take their choice."

Here I lost my reverence completely, and protested against any theory of the sort, because, to me at least, Tom Sawyer was real.

"Oh, he is real," said Mark Twain. "He's all the boy that I have known or recollect; but that would be a good way of ending the book"; then, turning round, "because, when you come to think of it, neither religion, training, nor education avails anything against the force of circumstances that drive a man. Suppose we took the next four and twenty years of Tom

Sawyer's life, and gave a little joggle to the circumstances that controlled him. He would logically and according to the joggle turn out a rip or an angel."

" Do you believe that, then? "

" I think so. Isn't it what you call kismet? "

" Yes; but don't give him two joggles and show the result, because he isn't your property any more. He belongs to us. "

Thereat he laughed—a large, wholesome laugh—and this began a dissertation on the rights of a man to do what he liked with his own creations, which being a matter of purely professional interest, I will mercifully omit.

Returning to the big chair, he, speaking of truth and the like in literature, said that an autobiography was the one work in which a man, against his own will and in spite of his utmost striving to the contrary, revealed himself in his true light to the world.

" A good deal of your life on the

125

Mississippi is autobiographical, isn't
it?" I asked.

"As near as it can be—when a man
is writing to a book and about himself.
But in genuine autobiography, I believe it is impossible for a man to tell
the truth about himself or to avoid
impressing the reader with the truth
about himself.

"I made an experiment once. I got
a friend of mine—a man painfully giv-
en to speak the truth on all occasions—
a man who wouldn't dream of telling a
lie—and I made him write his autobiography for his own amusement and
mine. He did it. The manuscript
would have made an octavo volume,
but—good, honest man that he was—in
every single detail of his life that I
knew about he turned out, on paper, a
formidable liar. He could not help
himself.

"It is not in human nature to write
the truth about itself. None the less
the reader gets a general impression
from an autobiography whether the

man is a fraud or a good man. The reader can't give his reasons any more than a man can explain why a woman struck him as being lovely when he doesn't remember her hair, eyes, teeth, or figure. And the impression that the reader gets is a correct one."

"Do you ever intend writing an autobiography?"

"If I do, it will be as other men have done—with the most earnest desire to make myself out to be the better man in every little business that has been to my discredit; and I shall fail, like the others, to make the readers believe anything except the truth."

This naturally led to a discussion on conscience. Then said Mark Twain, and his words are mighty and to be remembered:

"Your conscience is a nuisance. A conscience is like a child. If you pet it and play with it and let it have everything that it wants, it becomes spoiled and intrudes on all your amusements and most of your griefs.

127

Treat your conscience as you would treat anything else. When it is rebellious, spank it—be severe with it, argue with it, prevent it from coming to play with you at all hours, and you will secure a good conscience; that is to say, a properly trained one. A spoiled one simply destroys all the pleasure in life. I think I have reduced mine to order. At least, I haven't heard from it for some time. Perhaps I have killed it from over-severity. It's wrong to kill a child, but, in spite of all I have said, a conscience differs from a child in many ways. Perhaps it's best when it's dead."

Here he told me a little—such things as a man may tell a stranger—of his early life and upbringing, and in what manner he had been influenced for good by the example of his parents. He spoke always through his eyes, a light under the heavy eyebrows; anon crossing the room with a step as light as a girl's, to show me some book or other; then resuming his walk up and

down the room, puffing at the cob pipe.
I would have given much for nerve
enough to demand the gift of that pipe
—value, five cents when new. I understood why certain savage tribes
ardently desired the liver of brave men
slain in combat. That pipe would have
given me, perhaps, a hint of his keen
insight into the souls of men. But he
never laid it aside within stealing reach
of my arms.

Once, indeed, he put his hand on my
shoulder. It was an investiture of the
Star of India, blue silk, trumpets, and
diamond-studded jewel, all complete.
If hereafter, in the changes and
chances of this mortal life, I fall to
cureless ruin, I will tell the superin-
tendent of the workhouse that Mark
Twain once put his hand on my shoulder, and he shall give me a room to
myself and a double allowance of pau-
pers' tobacco.

"I never read novels myself," said
he, "except when the popular persecution forces me to—when people plague

me to know what I think of the last
book that every one is reading."

"And how did the latest persecution
affect you?"

"Robert?" said he interrogatively.

I nodded.

"I read it, of course, for the work-
manship. That made me think I had
neglected novels too long—that there
might be a good many books as graceful in style somewhere on the shelves;
so I began a course of novel reading.
I have dropped it now; it did not
amuse me. But as regards Robert, the
effect on me was exactly as though a
singer of street ballads were to hear
excellent music from a church organ.,
I didn't stop to ask whether the music
was legitimate or necessary. I listened, and I liked what I heard. I am
speaking of the grace and beauty of
the style."

How is one to behave when one
differs altogether with a great man?
My business was to be still and to listen. Yet Mark—Mark Twain, a man

who knew men—"big Injun, heap big
Injun, dam mighty heap big Injun"
—master of tears and mirth, skilled in
wisdom of the true inwardness of
things—was bowing his head to the
labored truck of the schools where men
act in obedience to the books they read
and keep their consciences in spirits
of homemade wine. He said the style
was graceful; therefore it must be
graceful. But perhaps he was making
fun of me. In either case I would lay
my hand upon my mouth.

"You see," he went on, "every man
has his private opinion about a book.
But that is my private opinion. If I
had lived in the beginning of things, I
should have looked around the town-
ship to see what popular opinion
thought of the murder of Abel before
I openly condemned Cain. I should
have had my private opinion, of
course, but I shouldn't have expressed
it until I had felt the way. You have
my private opinion about that book.
I don't know what my public ones

are exactly. They won't upset the earth."

He recurled himself into the chair and talked of other things.

"I spend nine months of the year at Hartford. I have long ago satisfied myself that there is no hope of doing much work during those nine months. People come in and call. They call at all hours, about everything in the world. One day I thought I would keep a list of interruptions. It began this way:

"A man came and would see no one but Mr. Clemens. He was an agent for photogravure reproductions of salon pictures. I very seldom use salon pictures in my books.

"After that man another man, who refused to see any one but Mr. Clemens, came to make me write to Washington about something. I saw him. I saw a third man, then a fourth. By this time it was noon. I had grown tired of keeping the list. I wished to rest.

"But the fifth man was the only one

of the crowd with a card of his own.
He sent up his card. ' Ben Koontz,
Hannibal, Mo.' I was raised in Hannibal. Ben was an old schoolmate of
mine. Consequently I threw the house
wide open and rushed with both hands
out at a big, fat, heavy man, who was
not the Ben I had ever known—nor
anything like him.

"'But is it you, Ben?' I said.
'You've altered in the last thousand
years.'

"The fat man said: ' Well, I'm not
Koontz exactly, but I met him down in
Missouri, and he told me to be sure
and call on you, and he gave me his
card, and'— here he acted the little
scene for my benefit—' if you can wait
a minute till I can get out the circulars
—I'm not Koontz exactly, but I'm
travelling with the fullest line of rods
you ever saw.' "

"And what happened?" I asked
breathlessly.

"I shut the door. He was not Ben
Koontz—exactly—not my old school-

fellow, but I had shaken him by both hands in love, and . . . I had been bearded by a lightning-rod man in my own house.

"As I was saying, I do very little work in Hartford. I come here for three months every year, and I work four or five hours a day in a study down the garden of that little house on the hill. Of course, I do not object to two or three interruptions. When a man is in the full swing of his work these little things do not affect him. Eight or ten or twenty interruptions retard composition."

I was burning to ask him all manner of impertinent questions, as to which of his works he himself preferred, and so forth; but, standing in awe of his eyes, I dared not. He spoke on, and I listened grovelling.

It was a question of mental equipment that was on the carpet, and I am still wondering whether he meant what he said.

"Personally I never care for fiction

or story books. What I like to read about are facts and statistics of any kind. If they are only facts about the raising of radishes, they interest me. Just now, for instance, before you came in "—he pointed to an encyclopædia on the shelves—" I was reading an article about ' Mathematics.' Perfectly pure mathematics.

" My own knowledge of mathematics stops at ' twelve times twelve,' but I enjoyed that article immensely. I didn't understand a word of it; but facts, or what a man believes to be facts, are always delightful. That mathematical fellow believed in his facts. So do I. Get your facts first, and "—the voice dies away to an almost inaudible drone—" then you can distort 'em as much as you please."

Bearing this precious advice in my bosom, I left, the great man assuring me with gentle kindness that I had not interrupted him in the least. Once outside the door, I yearned to go back and ask some questions—it was easy

enough to think of them now—but his
time was his own, though his books
belonged to me.

I should have ample time to look
back to that meeting across the graves
of the days. But it was sad to think
of the things he had not spoken about.

In San Francisco the men of *The
Call* told me many legends of Mark's
apprenticeship in their paper five and
twenty years ago; how he was a reporter delightfully incapable of report-
ing according to the needs of the day.
He preferred, so they said, to coil
himself into a heap and meditate until
the last minute. Then he would produce copy bearing no sort of relation-
ship to his legitimate work—copy that
made the editor swear horribly, and
the readers of *The Call* ask for more.

I should like to have heard Mark's
version of that and some stories of his
joyous and variegated past. He has
been journeyman printer (in those
days he wandered from the banks of
the Missouri even to Philadelphia), pi-

lot cub and full-blown pilot, soldier of the South (that was for three weeks only), private secretary to a Lieutenant-Governor of Nevada (that displeased him), miner, editor, special correspondent in the Sandwich Islands, and the Lord only knows what else. If so experienced a man could by any means be made drunk, it would be a glorious thing to fill him up with composite liquors, and, in the language of his own country, "let him retrospect." But these eyes will never see that orgy fit for the gods.

RUDYARD KIPLING.

VII

THE KIPLING BOOKS.

Following is a reference list of the books written by Rudyard Kipling:

I.

QUARTETTE. CHRISTMAS ANNUAL. 8vo, pp. 125. Lahore. 1885.

II.

ON HER MAJESTY'S SERVICE ONLY. DEPARTMENTAL DITTIES. Oblong 8vo. Lahore. 1886.

III.

PLAIN TALES FROM THE HILLS. 12mo. pp. 283. Calcutta and London. 1888.

IV.

SOLDIERS THREE. 12mo, pp. 97. Allahabad. 1888.

THE KIPLING BOOKS.

V.

THE STORY OF THE GADSBYS. 12mo,
pp. 100. Allahabad. N. D. (1888.)

VI.

IN BLACK AND WHITE. 12mo, pp. 106,
Allahabad. N. D. (1888.)

VII.

UNDER THE DEODARS, 12mo, pp. 106
Allahabad. N. D. (1888.)

VIII.

THE PHANTOM 'RICKSHAW AND OTHER
TALES. 12mo, pp. 104. Allahabad. N.
D. (1888.)

IX.

WEE WILLIE WINKIE AND OTHER
STORIES. 12mo, pp. 96. Allahabad. N.
D. (1888.)

X.

THE COURTING OF DINAH SHADD AND
OTHER STORIES. 12mo, pp. 182.
New York. 1890.

XI.

DEPARTMENTAL DITTIES AND OTHER
VERSES. 12mo, pp. 121. Calcutta, London and Bombay. 1891.

139

XII.

THE CITY OF DREADFUL NIGHT. 12mo,
pp. 96. Allahabad. N. D. (1891.)

XIII.

LIFE'S HANDICAP. STORIES OF MINE
OWN PEOPLE. 12mo, pp. 351. London
and New York. 1891.

XIV.

LETTERS OF MARQUE. 8vo, pp. 154.
Allahabad. 1891.

XV.

BARRACK-ROOM BALLADS AND OTHER
VERSES. 12mo, pp. 208. London. 1892.

XVI.

THE NAULAHKA. A STORY OF WEST
AND EAST. 12mo, pp. 276. London and
New York. 1892.

XVII.

BALLADS AND BARRACK-ROOM BAL-
LADS. 12mo, pp. 207. New York and London. 1892.

XVIII.

MANY INVENTIONS. 12mo, pp. 365. London and New York. 1893.

THE KIPLING BOOKS.

XIX.

THE JUNGLE BOOK. 12mo, pp. 212. London and New York. 1894.

XX.

THE SECOND JUNGLE BOOK. 12mo, pp. 238. London and New York. 1895.

XXI.

THE SEVEN SEAS. 12mo. London and New York. 1896.

XXII.

SLAVES OF THE LAMP. 12mo. London and New York. 1897.

XXIII.

CAPTAINS COURAGEOUS. 12mo, pp. 387. New York and London. 1897.

XXIV.

THE DAY'S WORK. 12mo. New York and London. 1898.

XXV.

A FLEET IN BEING. London. 1899.

XXVI.

STALKY & COMPANY. 12mo. London and New York. 1899.